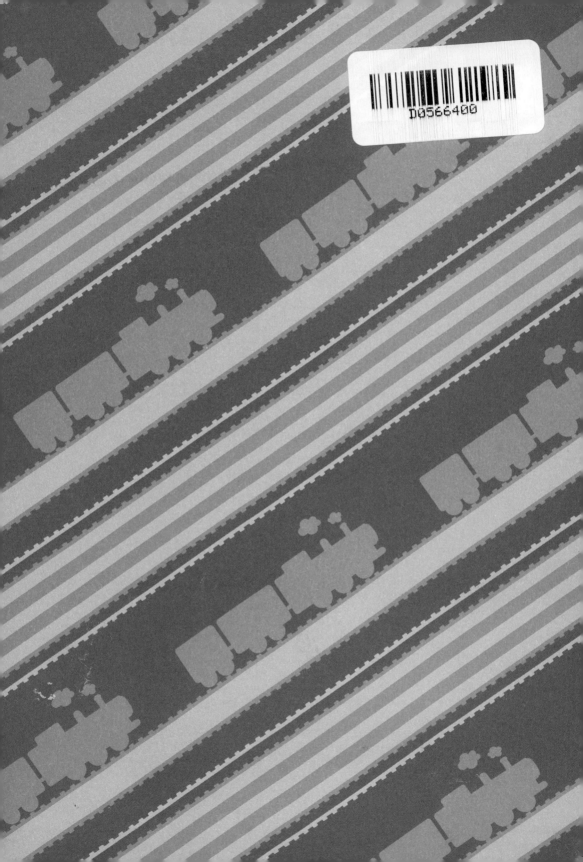

Thomas the Tank Engine & Friends™

CREATED BY BRITT ALLCROFT

Based on The Railway Series by The Reverend W Awdry.
© 2009 Gullane (Thomas) LLC.
Thomas the Tank Engine & Friends and Thomas & Friends are trademarks of Gullane
(Thomas) Limited. Thomas the Tank Engine & Friends & Design is Reg. U.S. Pat. & Tm. Off.
HIT and the HIT Entertainment logo are trademarks of HIT Entertainment Limited.
All rights reserved. Published in the United States by Random House Children's Books,
a division of Random House, Inc., New York, and in Canada by
Random House of Canada Limited, Toronto.
Bright and Early Books and colophon and Random House and colophon
are registered trademarks of Random House, Inc.

HiT entertainment

Visit us on the Web!
www.thomasandfriends.com   www.randomhouse.com/kids/thomas

Library of Congress Cataloging-in-Publication Data
Stubbs, Tommy. Fast train, slow train / illustrated by Tommy Stubbs. — 1st ed.
p. cm. — (Bright and early books)
"Thomas the Tank Engine & Friends created by Britt Allcroft,
based on The Railway Series by The Reverend W Awdry."
Summary: In this version of the "Tortoise and the Hare" fable,
two train engines compete in a race.
ISBN 978-0-375-85689-1 (trade) — ISBN 978-0-375-95689-8 (lib. bdg.)
[1. Stories in rhyme. 2. Railroad trains—Fiction. 3. Racing—Fiction.
4. Pride and vanity—Fiction.] I. Awdry, W. Railway series. II. Title.
PZ8.3.S9223Fas 2009   [E]—dc22   2008016717
Printed in the United States of America
10 9 8 7 6   First Edition

Train,
Slow Train

Illustrated by Tommy Stubbs

A Bright and Early Book

From BEGINNER BOOKS®

A Division of Random House, Inc.

James is off to Ballahoo.
Edward has to go there, too.

James thinks that he's so fine—
the fastest racer on the line.
James says he wants to race.
Edward makes a funny face.

James sets off.
Go, go, go!

Edward follows—
so, so slow.

James races. Clickety-clack.
Edward chugs on down the track.

Look! A cow! James races past.
He's a racer, racing fast.

Edward slows down for the cow.
Does she need his help somehow?

Look! A calf is on the track.
Edward stops to get it back.

James races. Clickety-clack.
Edward chugs on down the track.

Look! It's Percy!
Stuck on the track.

James races on.
Edward holds back!

Edward helps a friend in need.

Racing James keeps the lead.

Bertie is stuck.
He is out of gas.
He needs help.
James races past.

Edward slows and
then he stops.

He takes some shoppers
to the shops.

James thinks he is the best.
He's way ahead. He can rest.
He sees that he is bright and clean
in his reflection in the stream.

James thinks he is the better train.
Isn't he a little vain?

James does not see
Edward chug past.

But now it is James
who is the last.

Edward gets to Ballahoo.
He is slow and Really Useful, too.

James the racer lost the race.
Vanity won him second place.